Tamara Small and the
Monsters' Ball

by
Giles Paley-Phillips

illustrated by
Gabriele Antonini

The wind outside is **wailing**.

The wind it starts to howl.

The dog **hears** someone stirring

and he starts to **bark** and growl.

Tamara Small **feels** frightened
as she **lies awake** in bed.
She thinks that **something's** coming,
so she **tightly** clutches Ted.

Below **Tamara's** window,
there's a **shadow** moving **round**.
It is big and **really scary**
and it makes a **grizzly** sound.

Then, suddenly the window
bursts open with a **crash!**
A **hairy** arm comes in the room
and grabs her in a **flash.**

"Where are you taking me?"
Tamara cries in fear,
but the monster simply grunts a bit
and wipes away her tear.

Then out of the **darkness**
come **lots** and **lots** of creatures.
Tamara is quite **startled**
by their **funny**-looking features.

There are **goblins**, there are **ghosts**, there are **ghouls** and there are **bats**. There are **witches** up on broomsticks, wearing black and **pointy hats**.

ANNUAL MONSTERS' BALL

They're **all** heading down
to the **old village hall**,
where a **sign** above the door
says, 'Annual Monsters' Ball'.

Inside there are monsters **dancing**.
They **jive** and cha cha **cha**.
There's a **breakdancing** werewolf
whose moves are quite **bizarre!**

Soon Tamara's on the floor
and joining in the fun.
Before the night is over,
she has danced with everyone!

She then **lets** out a little yawn
as the **sun** begins to rise.
The witches start to cackle;
"We've got one last **surprise!"**

"For being great at dancing,
with moves that are sublime,
we've conjured up a special gift;
a cake made out of slime."

Then each and every creature
gives out a massive cheer;
"We really hope Tamara,
can come again next year!"

The witches cackle once again
and cast a magic spell
to take Tamara straight back home.
They bid a fond farewell.

Soon Tamara's fast asleep
and tucked up in her bed.
She's dreaming of the monsters' ball
while tightly clutching Ted.

The End

Tamara Small and the Monsters' Ball
is an original concept by
© Giles Paley-Phillips
Author : Giles Paley-Phillips

Illustrated by Gabriele Antonini
Gabriele Antonini is represented by
Advocate Art Ltd
www.advocate-art.com

A CIP catalogue record for this book
is available from the British Library.

**PUBLISHED BY MAVERICK ARTS
PUBLISHING LTD**
©Maverick Arts Publishing Limited

Studio 3A, City Business Centre, 6 Brighton Road,

Horsham, West Sussex, RH13 5BB

+44(0) 1403 256941

First Edition Published October 2012
This Edition Published May 2015

ISBN 978-1-84886-175-6

www.maverickbooks.co.uk